D1483566

PRAISE FOR
ANNA STRONG, VAMPIRE SERIES

HAUNTED

"Many unexpected twists and turns . . . Packed with action that is sure to chill readers to the bone."
—*Examiner.com*

"Fast-paced . . . Fans of the series will be stunned by this powerful, twisting thriller."
—*Midwest Book Review*

"Haunted offers true edge-of-your-seat drama . . . Buckle up, because megatalented Stein is heading into severely hazardous (and unputdownable) territory!"
—*RT Book Reviews* (4 ½ stars)

"Dynamic . . . Anna is what every urban fantasy heroine should be. A tough, gutsy, complex character who delivers what's promised."
—*Smexy Books*

"[Anna is] a badass, no-mercy kind of girl . . . If you want some kick-ass vampire in your life, this series is just for you!"
—*Under the Covers Book Blog*

DISCARDED
Bruce County Public Library
1243 MacKenzie Rd.
Port Elgin, Ontario N0H 2C6

CROSSROADS

"A kick-ass heroine readers will delight in . . . *Crossroads* will take readers on some twist[s] and turns that won't let you put this book down until the very end, and then you will be hungry for the next installment."

—*Fresh Fiction*

"[A] powerful novel . . . Stein continues to challenge her gutsy heroine, both emotionally and physically . . . Another for your must-read pile!"

—*RT Book Reviews* (4 ½ stars)

"I just love the character Anna. She has grown so much from the beginning, and I believe she is finally coming into her own in *Crossroads* . . . There were some surprises that I wasn't expecting . . . Make no mistake, Anna is growing into what she could become, and it is good to see. If you love strong female leads, then this series is for you."

—*Night Owl Reviews* (Top Pick)

CHOSEN

"With each book in the series, not only have Stein's characters become stronger but so has her writing . . . Hard-hitting urban fantasy with a hard-hitting female lead."

—*Fresh Fiction*

"From the opening chapter of this terrific series, Stein has sent her gutsy heroine on an uncharted journey filled with danger and bitter betrayal . . . In this pivotal but emotionally brutal book, skillful Stein reveals some critical answers and delivers some devastating blows. Like a fine wine, this series is improving with age. Brava!"

—*RT Book Reviews* (4 ½ stars)

RETRIBUTION

"The fifth book in the exceptional first-person Anna Strong series is a powerful entry in an amazing saga."
—*RT Book Reviews*

"Ms. Stein has a true gift in storytelling and continues to add exciting new elements to this well-built world. Retribution is an engrossing read with an action-packed story line and secondary characters that are every bit as intriguing as the heroine. This is a must-read for fans of the series!"
—*Darque Reviews*

LEGACY

"Urban fantasy with true depth and flair!"
—*RT Book Reviews* (4 ½ stars)

"As riveting as the rest . . . One of my favorite urban fantasy series."
—*Darque Reviews*

THE WATCHER

"Action fills every page, making this a novel that flies by . . . Dynamic relationships blend [with] complex mysteries in this thriller."
—*Huntress Book Reviews*

"An exciting, fast-paced novel . . . First-rate plotting."
—*LoveVampires*

"Dazzles readers with action-packed paranormal adventure, love and friendship. With many wonderfully executed twists and turns, this author's suspenseful writing will hold readers spellbound until the very end."
—*Darque Reviews*

"Snappy action and plot twists that will hold readers' interest to the last page."
—*Monsters and Critics*

BLOOD DRIVE

"Once again Jeanne C. Stein delivers a jam-packed story full of mystery and intrigue that will keep you glued to the edge of your seat! Just like [with] the first book in the Anna Strong series, *The Becoming*, I could not put this book down even for a second. You will find yourself cheering Anna on as she goes after the bad guys. Jeanne C. Stein has given us a wonderful tough-as-nails heroine everyone will love!"

—*Night Owl Reviews*

"Jeanne C. Stein takes on the vampire mythos in her own unique manner that makes for an enthralling vampire thriller. Readers of Laurell K. Hamilton, Tanya Huff and Charlaine Harris will thoroughly enjoy this fast-paced novel filled with several action scenes that come one after the other, making it hard for the readers to catch a breather."

—*Midwest Book Review*

THE BECOMING

"This is a really, really good book. Anna is a great character, Stein's plotting is adventurous and original, and I think most of my readers would have a great time with The Becoming."

—*Charlaine Harris*, #1 *New York Times* bestselling author of the Sookie Stackhouse novels

"With plot twists, engaging characters and smart writing, this first installment in a new supernatural series has all the marks of a hit. Anna Strong lives up to her name: equally tenacious and vulnerable, she's a heroine with the charm, savvy and intelligence that fans of Laurell K. Hamilton and Kim Harrison will be happy to root for . . . If this debut novel is any indication, Stein has a fine career ahead of her."

—*Publishers Weekly*

ANNA AND THE VAMPIRE PRINCE

ANNA AND THE VAMPIRE PRINCE

AN ANNA STRONG VAMPIRE NOVELLA

JEANNE C. STEIN

HEX PUBLISHERS

This is a work of fiction. All characters, organizations, and events portrayed in this book are products of the author's imagination and/or are used fictitiously.

ANNA AND THE VAMPIRE PRINCE

Copyright © 2015 by Jeanne C. Stein. All rights reserved.

Cover art by Kirk DouPonce
Cover design by Kirk DouPonce and Joshua Viola
Typesets and formatting by Dustin Carpenter

A Hex Publishers Book

Published & Distributed by Hex Publishers, LLC
PO BOX 298
Erie, CO 80516

www.HexPublishers.com

No portion of this book may be reproduced without first obtaining the permission of the copyright holder.

Cover art copyright © by Hex Publishers, LLC.
Hex Publishers TM is a trademark of Hex Publishers, LLC.

Joshua Viola, Publisher

Print ISBN-10: 0-9964039-6-5
Print ISBN-13: 978-0-9964039-6-2
Ebook ISBN-10: 0-9964039-7-3
Ebook ISBN-13: 978-0-9964039-7-9

First Hex Edition: 2017

Anna and the Vampire Prince previously published by ARe Books
January 2016

10 9 8 7 6 5 4 3 2 1

Printed in the U.S.A.

ACKNOWLEDGMENTS

FIRST, THANKS TO ALL OF ANNA'S FRIENDS AND supporters who wanted another story. Hope you enjoy this one. Second, thanks first to ARe and then to Hex Publishers and Josh Viola for making this available. And third, thanks to my critique group. Without them, this writing game would be much harder.

ONE

I AWAKE WITH A START. BELOW MY BEDROOM
window, indistinct chatter, male and female, floats up. It's the
work crew, awaiting instructions. Waiting for my dad.

I listen for a moment, then roll over and do what I've done
every day since Frey and John-John left. Reach out a hand to
the empty space beside me in bed.

I'm still here in France. It's been three weeks since Mom
died. Two since Frey and John-John went back to Monu-
ment Valley. I know we'd agreed that John-John would go
to school on the reservation so he wouldn't lose touch with
his roots—or his grandparents. That they'd spend summers
and breaks in San Diego. But I miss them both more than I
thought possible.

I stretch and yawn. I *could* go back to San Diego. Dad
and Trish don't really need me here. But neither do David
and Tracey in San Diego. They're running the business, and
according to Tracey, it's going as well as can be expected given
the circumstances. She was madly in love with David but he

has rekindled his relationship with Gloria. I feel responsible for that, since in the glow of wedded bliss, I encouraged him to follow his heart. Tracey says she's getting over him and David has had the good grace to keep Gloria away from the office.

Still…

My father's voice drifts up now, silencing the din from below, giving instructions to the work crew about what needs to be done in spring to protect the grape harvest. Today they'll be going through the fields trellising, pruning, weeding. Looking for disease signs and for cane borer damage. Feeding, applying herbicides, checking irrigation systems.

Everything to assure a healthy growing cycle.

I smile. It's amazing how much he's learned in the short time he's owned the vineyard.

His voice is firm, unwavering. When he's finished with instructions, I know he'll lead the crew to the fields. He's been working with them every day since Mom died.

I glance at the bedside clock. Five AM. Trish won't be up for another hour. I swing out of bed and reach for my robe. I'll go downstairs and start breakfast. Be there to see her off to school. Give her a hug and let her know how much she is loved.

Nothing, though, can replace the hole left by my mother's death. I hear Trish crying sometimes. I wish there was something I could do to ease the pain. But time is the only remedy.

For me, too. At some point, I have to leave. Get back to San Diego and jumpstart my own life.

But not today.

I'd be returning to an empty house.

I pad downstairs, cinching my robe tighter around my waist. A vampire is impervious to temperature, but even I feel the chill of early morning in Provence on my bare feet. The morning sun has yet to spill its warmth over the vineyards and inch its way to the house. Dad has already started the coffee so I pour myself a cup and take it outside.

The grounds on the estate are beautiful, lush. It's been a wet spring and the early blooming iris and wildflowers are a colorful backdrop to the cherry and apple trees, alive with their pale pink and snow white sprays on slender branches. In the distance stretch the vineyards, now teeming with life as the workers make their way through the even rows of new growth on century old stock. Rebirth.

A concept not unfamiliar to the vampire.

It reminds me that I have an appointment with Vlad at noon. I haven't fed since Frey left and the hunger is beginning to gnaw. Vlad is taking me to a place where I can fulfill that hunger safely.

I turn back to the kitchen. I can fulfill Trish's simple human hunger, too.

She likes pancakes.

That's what I'll make.

TWO

I'M EARLY FOR MY MEETING WITH VLAD AT A downtown café in Lorgues. It's an open-air café I've visited often, with Frey while he was here, with Dad and Trish after visits to the teeming farmer's market across the street. Now that spring is here, the transformation along the tree-lined streets is breathtaking. The once skeletal white trunks and branches are fully leafed, stretching a canopy of pale green from one side of the street to the other. Sunlight filters through the leaves, painting planters filled with hyacinths, poppies and the ubiquitous lavender a dappled golden hue.

I sip a cappuccino while I wait, pretending to be just another human basking in the warm afternoon sun. I close my eyes and tilt my head back—until the familiar growl of a Ducati brings a smile to my lips. The Harley was Vlad's vehicle of choice until he crashed it on a mountain road in the dead of night. A friend convinced him the Ducati was more suited to his driving and temperament, he, like the bike, being head-strong and speed driven.

He's still half a mile away but I reach out with my thoughts. *You just can't resist making an entrance, can you?*

There's no immediate response but I can feel his amusement. Vlad is the oldest vampire I've ever met. Maybe the oldest vampire in existence, and his power is astounding. When I first met him, I felt it—what the old one's called *gravitas*. Now we've become friends. A fact that still amazes me.

The Ducati rumbles to a stop in front of the café. Vlad's eyes are on me as he dismounts, but *he* has attracted the eyes of all the diners seated around me. He could be a model for *Vogue*. He's not handsome. His features are all angles and squares—rugged, wild. He's dressed in jeans and a red tee shirt underneath a black leather bomber. Short leather boots and black riding gloves complete the picture. He's the modern *Vogue* model. A bit unkempt. A bit untamed.

He's running a hand through his dark hair as he approaches, smoothing it away from a sculpted face in a casual, completely unself-conscious manner. If I didn't know him, I'd suspect it was an orchestrated move. But Vlad is the most unpretentious person I've ever met. I guess being on this earth almost six hundred years has stripped him of whatever vanity mortals are burdened with.

Which explains his reaction to my comment. He is always amused when anyone accuses him of doing anything to attract attention to himself, in spite of his loud motorcycle.

He plants a kiss on my cheek and then sits opposite me at the table, gesturing to a waiter, to my cup and then to himself. The waiter nods and disappears inside.

"Making an entrance?" he says. "You know me better than that."

I jab a thumb at his Ducati. "Then you'd better put a muffler on that thing."

He laughs, clutching a hand to his chest. "And muzzle my beast?" He leans forward, smile disappearing. "How are you doing?"

I lift my shoulders. "Fine as can be expected. Mom's death is hardest on Trish and Dad…" I let my words drop.

Vlad places a hand briefly over mine, then withdraws it as the waiter brings his cappuccino. We sip for a few minutes in silence. Then I ask, "Where are we going today?"

Vlad leans back in his chair. "A little place right outside of town. A chateau owned by a friend of mine. I let him know we were coming so he'll be prepared."

"You did tell him I want only the blood, right? Nothing else."

Vlad nods. "Of course. I told him you were a newlywed and faithful to your vows."

His words have a hint of amusement and something else. Mockery?

"Are you making fun of me?" I bristle.

"Of course not. You are a relatively new vampire."

"Which means?"

"Which means you haven't been around long enough yet to fully understand how different your life is from a mortal's. Someday human values won't mean that much to you."

I lower my head and pretend to focus on my cup, but really, I'm trying to digest what Vlad just said. "You mean values like honor, loyalty, respect. Commitment." I raise my eyes to meet his. "I can't imagine a time when I won't hold human values important. I'm a little disappointed that you'd suggest I would."

"I've offended you." Vlad's tone is abrupt. "I'm sorry. You may be the exception to the rule. I hope you are."

"I thought you were, too," I answer softly.

"Maybe. I know it wasn't always so." He drains his cup, reaches into his pocket and throws some Euros on the table. "Are you ready to go?"

I push away and stand up, glad to be done with this conversation. "Do you want to take my car?" I ask. "It's just around the corner."

But he's already started toward his bike. *No. The bike is faster and I know where we're going.*

He's switched to communicating with me telepathically. I follow him to the street and wait until he's mounted the bike to slip behind him. He's revving the engine so I wrap my arms securely around his waist and press my face into the back of his jacket.

He guns the Ducati aggressively into the street, and if I hadn't been prepared, I'd have been left bouncing on my ass in the middle of the road.

Over the thirty minutes it takes us to reach our destination, I try a couple of times to read his thoughts, but they're locked down tight. So I give up and enjoy springtime in the countryside outside Lorgues. It's rolling and lush with new spring growth. The fields of lavender haven't started to bloom here yet, but the promise is there.

Vlad turns left off the main road onto what looks like a long, paved driveway. In a short while, we approach a house. In the way of the french, Vlad called it a chateau, but it's really not much more than a cottage tucked under big shade trees on a lot dotted with flower gardens. We leave the bike on the driveway, and he leads the way to the front door.

It opens before either of us can knock.

A woman greets us with a smile. She grabs Vlad by the shoulders and gives him a peck on both cheeks before planting a lingering kiss on his lips.

When she finally lets him go, she turns sparkling eyes on me. "Bonjour. Bienvenue chez moi!"

"Better use English," Vlad says with a laugh. *Or this.*

"Je parle un peu le français, vous savez," I tell him. *But very little so this is probably best. I'm Anna Strong,"* I add, holding out my hand.

She takes it. "Amélie," she responds.

Amélie gestures us inside. She's tall and lean and has beautiful auburn hair. She's dressed in a long silk tunic and is barefoot. Since she's vampire, I can't guess how long she's been on this earth, but I'd guess her human age at turning to be thirty.

Thirty-one, she corrects me. *And thank you for the compliment. Would you like some tea before you feed?*

Vlad speaks up before I can respond. *No. We don't have that much time. I have to get back.*

That Marseilles business? she asks.

Yes.

She makes clucking noises with her tongue. *I'm sorry.* She turns to me. *Right this way, ma chère.*

Vlad calls to her as we leave the room. "Where is Alexander?"

"In the study. He's expecting you."

Amélie leads me to a room off the end of a long hallway. She swings open the door. *Take as much time as you need. Georges knows what to expect.*

I wish that I did. It's the first time I've been offered a host here in France. Back at home, if Frey isn't with me, I head for Beso de la Muerte where my friend Culebra is my provider. There are no surprises there. I don't know when I'll be heading back home, though, and the urge to feed is becoming paramount.

The man, Georges, lies on his back on a bed in a sunny, cheerful room. Amélie closes the door behind me and he rolls toward me. His eyes meet mine.

"You are American? My name is Georges."

Thankfully, he's fully dressed. I nod and make a motion with my hand and he rolls again so his back is to me. When I feed from a male, I prefer this position. I don't have to feel his obvious physical reaction to the feeding.

George has unbuttoned his shirt and now he pulls it off his shoulders and offers me his neck. I settle myself beside him, an arm across his chest, and let my lips graze his neck. He shudders and I know it's not from fear, but from excitement. Humans who offer themselves as hosts take great pleasure from the act.

When I break the skin at the carotid, just at the base of his neck, he moans and shifts to press himself closer. I draw first blood, the clean, sweet and salty elixir that sustains my life. As it courses through me, every cell comes alive. For a vampire, only feeding and sex impart warmth. This is the most human I've felt since Frey left. The feeling will fade as soon as I'm finished, so I bask in it now.

Too soon, I know it's time to stop. I lick the wound, and Georges' artery and skin knit closed. I gently pull his shirt up over his shoulders.

"Combien vais-je vous payer?" I ask.

He looks surprised. "Rien. Nothing. I do it as a favor to my great friends Amélie and Alexander. It is my pleasure."

I nod. "Thank you."

He settles onto the bed. "I will sleep now for a little while."

I can't help but smile. The bulge in his slacks tells me he'll be doing something else first.

I leave him and return to the living room where Amélie awaits me. "Did it go well?" she asks.

"Perfectly. Thank you." I look around. "Vlad?"

"Still with Alexander."

Then she adds, *They should be finished shortly. Here, sit with me. Tell me about yourself.*

I join her on a chintz-covered couch. The room is decorated with rose wallpaper. Vases of flowers from the gardens outside mingle with books and knickknacks scattered over the surfaces of well-worn tables. Their scent mingles with fresh, spring air wafting through open windows. A fireplace mantle displays a bank of candles.

A very romantic room, I tell her.

Alexander and I are a very romantic couple.

How long have you been together?

Too many years to count. We met during the time of the great French revolution. A terrible, frightening time, but not all was lost. I found my soulmate. She fixes me with bright eyes. *Vlad tells me that you have, too.*

I drop my eyes. *Frey is a shifter, not vampire. We will not have centuries. But I believe that, yes, he is my soulmate.*

Then enjoy the time you have.

I smile. *We do.*

A door opens from somewhere down the hall. I expect Georges to appear, but instead it's Vlad. He's alone.

"Are you ready to go?" he asks.

The abrupt manner is back. "Yes."

He bends to Amélie and kisses her cheek. *Merci ma chère.*

Then he leans close and whispers in her ear telepathically. Too softly for even my vampiric hearing to pick up. Her brows furrow and her lips turn down in a frown. She whispers back and Vlad straightens.

I will be sure to keep you both informed, he tells her.

During this exchange, I'm left standing by the door, bristling over being left out. Their brief conversation may have been personal and none of my business, but my spidey senses are tingling. I wait until we're outside and on the Harley to ask, "What was that all about?"

He busies himself with the ignition and the bike roars to life. *Nothing.*

I wrap my arms around him and flash on something Amélie said when we first came in. "Does it have to do with what Amélie asked you earlier? Something about *the Marseilles business?*"

Vlad stiffens against my arms. *You have no power here, Anna,* he snaps. *You may be the Chosen One amongst your brethren, but here you are merely another vampire. Under my rule. Don't presume to interfere in matters that don't concern you.*

The rebuff stings me into silence. Until this moment, Vlad has treated me like an equal. I swallow back an angry reply and block my next thought from even his powerful mind.

Vlad steers the bike toward the street. He feels my anger and his bearing softens. *Really, Anna, it is of no importance to you. You have your family to think about, don't you?*

I let myself relax against him. *True. But I am here and as powerful a vampire as Amélie. You know you can trust me.*

He starts to say something else, I read the hesitation in his mind. But finally, he shakes his head. *I will keep that in mind,* is all he lets come through.

THREE

AT DINNER TONIGHT, TRISH IS BUBBLING WITH
good news. She and her best friend won parts in the spring
play at school. This is the most animated I've seen her since
Mom died and it's a balm to my soul.

Dad is equally impressed. "Trish, your grandmother
would be so proud!"

He's passing a platter of spring lamb and vegetables.
Smells delicious but I, of course, beg off with the excuse of a
late lunch in town. Dinner is always the hardest meal to fake.
I sip my wine and watch them eat.

"Your French must be superb," I tell Trish. "I can't believe
how quickly you've picked up the language."

"Well," she says modestly. "We have been here a few years
now. And Grandmother always practiced with me."

There's a wistful tone in her voice. Dad quickly chimes
in. "Well, if you need help with your lines, I'm here. Je parle
assez bien français, aussi, vous savez."

"Oui, vous le faites, pépé. Nous vous remercions de l'offre. Je vais vous prendre au mot."

They're grinning like Cheshire cats at each other. I flash again on the thought that maybe it's time for me to go back to San Diego. My work here may be done.

Then, I remember what happened with Vlad this afternoon. I can speak a little French, but not read it. "Dad? Is there anything in the newspaper about something going on in Marseilles?"

"Marseilles?" He pauses, eyebrows raised. "Nothing out of the ordinary in the last couple of days. But there is a perennial gang problem. Poverty, a large immigrant population, drugs. Just the right ingredients for a troubled community. A year ago, there were twenty drive-by shootings." He hands Trish a dish, then adds, "They call Marseilles the Gangland of the Riviera. Like Chicago in the 30's. Why do you ask?"

I take another sip of wine. "I just heard something in the café today."

"About the kidnappings?" Trish asks.

I look at her. "Kidnappings?"

Her expression is solemn. "Three in the last six months. Young girls. Taken right from their parents' homes. One girl was from Lorgues. I didn't know her, but my friend did. It's awful."

"Yes, that's right," Dad adds. "Two of the girls were found dead within three days of their disappearances. The third," he glances at Trish, "is still missing. She didn't go to your school, did she?"

Trish shakes her head. "No. But it's got everyone rattled anyway, especially since my friend Cecily knew her."

"And the Marseilles gangs are somehow involved?"

Dad shrugs. "No one knows for sure. But the girls were found in the northern part of the city, where gang activity is most prevalent. The motive seems to be ransom, but both parents of the dead girls paid and their daughters were still killed. It's a grim situation the police can't seem able to get a handle on."

My brain immediately gravitates to wondering if this could be something other than human dirtbags. Could there be a supernatural connection? Of course, asking if any of the girls were drained of their blood would hardly be a logical question to throw out.

A cell phone chimes from the other room. "That's probably Cecily," Trish says, brightening. "We've got to decide on our rehearsal schedule. Do you mind?" she asks Dad.

He waves her off. "Go. Can't interfere with the artist at work."

Once she's left, I smile at Dad. "She's really doing well." I lean closer and touch his hand. "How about you? How are you doing?"

The smile is still on his lips but his eyes cloud with sadness. "I miss your mother every minute of every day. I just thank God for you and Trish. Without you two…"

He must read something in my expression because he stops. He squeezes my hand. "It's time for you to go home, isn't it? Back to San Diego."

I release a breath. "You know I'll stay as long as you and Trish need me. But yes, at some point, I have to go back. David and Tracey have been carrying on without me but I can't ask them to do it forever."

He nods and sighs. "If it were up to me, I'd have you and Frey and John-John move here. Help me run the vineyard." He sighs again. "But that's my dream. Not yours. Your mother and I learned our lesson a long time ago about interfering—I won't make that mistake again."

He's speaking of the rift that once arose between us because I made the decision to give up teaching for bounty hunting. But that was another lifetime ago. Before I became vampire. Before Trish came into our lives. "That seems so long ago," I say.

"Not so long that I haven't forgotten the pain we caused you. I don't ever want you to resent me, Anna. Not ever again."

Trish bounds back into the room. She must sense the darkened mood because she stops, looking from her grandfather to me. "Is everything all right?"

"Absolutely." I gesture for her to return to her place at the table. "So when is this play anyway?"

"Three weeks." She slips into her chair. "We'll be rehearsing every day after school and on Saturday afternoons." She looks at Dad. "That's all right, isn't it? I promise to keep up with my chores and homework."

"Of course it is." He glances at me. "But I'm not sure your Aunt Anna will be here—"

"Are you kidding?" I stop him with an upturned hand. "Miss Trish's stage debut? Not on your life. David and Tracey can wait another couple of weeks." I lean toward Trish. "But I think you'd better translate the play for me before the curtain goes up. I don't think my limited French is up to the task."

It's not until later, when I'm in bed, that I think again about Vlad and his *Marseilles* problem. I don't know what's more aggravating, the way he shut me down or the fact that I'm so out of touch with the European vampire community. As he took great pleasure in reminding me, the vampires here, the oldest in existence, claim their own sovereignty. They never recognized my position as the Chosen One. Since the execution of their leader a few months ago, Vlad has reluctantly assumed a leadership role.

But then, I'm out of touch with my own vampire community. I've not had contact with any vampires, in the states to otherwise, and they, out of consideration for my mother's passing, have left me to grieve in private. That, too, will end once I return to the states.

My thoughts return to Marseille. Of course, there's the distinct possibility that the kidnappings have nothing to do with vampires. Not that anyone would admit if they suspected it might. Our existence is still a secret and most mortals know nothing of us.

Still, I'll go into town tomorrow and pick up an English edition newspaper. Maybe I can pick up a clue or two on my own.

FOUR

I LEAVE RIGHT AFTER BREAKFAST TO HEAD INTO
Lourges. I drop Trish off at school first and make a stop at a
little newsstand on Boulevard Georges Clemenceau, right next
to the café where I met Vlad yesterday. I find several English
language newspapers but pick *The Connexion*, a newspaper for
the ex-pat community in France. It's edited in Nice so I figure
it would have the most local news for the region.

Settled in at the café with a latte and the newspaper, it
doesn't take me long to find an article about the kidnappings.
During the night, the body of the third kidnap victim was
discovered. Strangled, just like the others, and killed after
the ransom demand had been met. I flash on Trish saying
last night that her friend had known the girl. It makes this
kidnapping feel very close to home.

The article goes on to say that it is believed an immigrant
gang is responsible, operating outside of Marseille. The suspicion is causing widespread resentment among the populace
toward those now working the vineyards. To make matters

worse, the leader of the gang is suspected to be Muslim. Police fear retaliation against all immigrants if the crimes are not solved quickly.

I take another sip of my coffee.

Well, that's certainly qualifies as "a Marseilles business." But nowhere does the article say that the girls met their deaths by exsanguination—which would suggest to me that these girls may have been killed by vampires. Of course, police have been known to keep certain facts about a crime from the public. But the cause of death in all three cases was listed as strangulation.

If I were in San Diego now, I could call a friend in the coroner's office and bribe him for more details.

As it is, all I can do is scan through the rest of the paper for anything else that might have a negative tie, however nebulous, to the vampire community. But I find no reports of attacks where a victim was bitten, no reports of animals found drained of their blood, no hospital or blood bank break-ins where blood was stolen. Nothing.

I fold up the paper, pay my bill, and head back to the estate.

———◆●●◆———

Trish is somber when she returns from school in the afternoon. The news of the dead girl, Elizabeth Garnier, spread quickly throughout her class. It had been especially hard on Cecily, who organized a letter writing campaign of condolence notes to be sent to the Garnier family. Somehow the media got wind of it, and television crews were on campus to watch the collection of the notes. Cecily was even interviewed for a spot on the evening news. We watch while eating dinner on TV trays so we won't miss the spot. Thanks to English close-captioning, I don't have to constantly interrupt to have Dad or Trish translate.

Cecily Gerard, a sweet-faced girl with bright blue eyes and honey blonde hair, is composed as she reads the note she's sending to her friend's family. She speaks of her sorrow and shares a story of friendship with the girl. She closes the note with a sincere hope that her note, and the notes of others, will offer some peace to the family.

Trish is crying as the interview comes to a close. Dad and I swipe at threatening tears ourselves. Maybe because death had been a recent visitor to our family, we feel a particular kinship with this girl's.

The notes won't take away any of the pain, but the knowledge that there are others who understand might help ease the burden a bit.

The rest of the newscast centers on the police inquiry and the growing antagonism sweeping the Marseille area toward the immigrant population. The police were doing their best to quell the animosity, but until they catch the killers, everyone who speaks a different language is suspect.

"That's not a good sign," I mumble as the news program drew to an end.

Dad is gathering the dinner dishes from our trays. "No. I wonder everyday if my French workers are going to start showing some hostility toward the immigrants working for me. I'd hate to see that."

"Why can't they catch the killers?" Trish asks. "The police must have some idea who's behind it."

"I'm sure they're doing their best." I squeeze her shoulders. "But in the meantime, you *are* careful about talking to strangers, right? And you don't go wandering off alone, even on the schoolyard, do you?"

"Aunt Anna," she snaps. "I'm not a child, you know."

But there is something else behind her words. Knowledge. Trish's childhood was marred by a monster of a mother who pimped her out to men for money. She's come a long way from that horrific time, but it will always be a part of her psyche.

"I know you're not a child," I whisper. "But neither were those girls."

Trish starts to reply but her cell phone chimes. She glances at the caller ID. "It's Cecily. I'll take it in my room."

I can see she's relieved to get away. I finish clearing the dishes and join Dad in the kitchen.

"Where's Trish?" Dad asks.

"She was saved from the clutches of an over-protective aunt by a telephone call. She's up in her room." I stack the dishes on the counter. "I'll wash if you dry."

Dad moves aside so I can fill the sink with hot, soapy water.

"Be careful," he says, watching steam rise. "You'll burn yourself."

I can't tell him I'm impervious to heat and cold so I dutifully add a little cold water to the mix.

While we're doing the dishes, he says, "I must admit, I'm more than a little nervous about what's happening in Marseille. The French have a name for where most immigrants live, *banelieu défavorisée,* poor areas that are considered by other residents as lawless or outside the law. Even the government is more comfortable letting them settle things on their own terms. A throwback to the time when the Mafia ran Marseille."

"The Mafia? You don't think of the Mafia as being a French thing."

"Ran the city for decades." He shrugs. "After a recent drive-by shooting, a local shopkeeper was heard to say that despite the bloodshed, he doesn't live in fear for himself or his business. The bad guys here know how to aim, he said. They never hit customers."

"Why are the police so sure it's an immigrant gang taking the girls?"

"Because they're a convenient target. Half the locals believe France should never have let foreigners into the country." Dad puts the finishing touch on the last of the silverware and dries his hands. "Of course, we who run vineyards would be lost without immigrant workers. The ones I have are hard-working, loyal and only trying to provide for their families."

"Have you received any threats?" I ask.

But before he can answer, Trish joins us in the kitchen. Her face, freshly scrubbed of tears, is still somber.

"You're timing is impeccable," I tell her. "We just finished the dishes."

But she doesn't smile. "Sorry."

"How is Cecily?" Dad asks.

Her shoulders raise in a half-shrug. "She's not sure she'll be at school tomorrow. She and her mom are taking the letters to Elizabeth's parents."

"Then I'll drive you tomorrow morning," I say. "And I'll pick you up from school, too."

She shoots me a *really?* look.

But she doesn't voice an objection.

It's just as well. It would have done her no good.

Trish's school is just outside the city boundaries—it's a Catholic school, a big, brick multi-level monstrosity run by the Jesuits. At three, she's waiting for me. I pull into the driveway behind a line of cars that stretches back to the street. Across the street, two police cars are stationed. Four officers are keeping an eye on the students.

"I don't remember there ever being this many parents picking up students," I comment, navigating around the jam.

"This is new," she says. "As are the police over there." What she doesn't add, what she has no need to add, is that it's because of the kidnappings.

"Did Cecily make it to school?"

Trish shakes her head. "She left a message on my cell that she'd see me tomorrow."

She's clutching her books to her chest like a lifeline.

"Do you have much homework?" I ask.

Another shake of the head.

"Then how about you and I go riding this afternoon? I'm sure the neighbors would welcome the help with horses."

Trish straightens a little in the seat. "You'll go with me?"

"If you don't take off like a bat out of hell and leave me in the dust."

Trish actually smiles. "I promise."

I don't tell Trish, but for that smile she could leave me anywhere she wanted.

———•••———

We get back from our horseback ride just as Dad is returning from his day in the vineyards.

He raises an eyebrow at me. "You look a little stiff."

Trish starts to laugh, hiding her face behind her hands.

I frown at her. "She rides like a racehorse jockey. I'm going to be sore for a week." Sad, but true. Even a vampire can feel the result of bouncing on a saddle for two hours.

He links arms with us. "Let's go into town for dinner," he says. "But you two need to shower first. You both smell like stable."

Trish races to the house while Dad and I follow behind at a more leisurely pace.

"Thank you for taking Trish riding," he says to me. "I can tell she enjoyed it."

"I did, too. Really." I rub my aching butt with the palm of my hand. "But my body isn't so happy."

We're at the front door when we hear the phone ringing inside. Dad steps through first and goes to the kitchen to answer it. In a minute, he's back, phone in hand, a deep frown darkening his face. He mouths at me, *Get Trish.*

The hair on the back of my neck starts to rise. I take the stairs two at a time, calling out for Trish as I go. She meets me in the hall in front of her bedroom door. She's wrapped in a robe.

"What's the matter?"

"Dad wants you downstairs."

I'm trying to keep panic from reflecting on my face and voice and evidently, failing.

Her expression soon mirrors what I'm feeling. "What's wrong?"

Dad's voice reaches us from the bottom of the stairs. "Come down, Trish."

She and I exchange a look of concern. Whatever it is, we both know, it's not good.

Dad has the phone in one hand when Trish and I get downstairs. He holds it out to Trish. "It's Cecily's mother. She needs to talk to you."

Trish takes the phone while Dad steers me a few steps away with a hand on my elbow. "Mrs. Gerard called for Cecily. She said her daughter left for school at noon and thought she planned to come home with Trish to go over lines for their play. At least that was the message she received from Cecily about two this afternoon. She was calling to see if she should come round to pick her up."

My heart plummets, remembering that Trish said Cecily left *her* a message that she wouldn't be at school at all. I look at Trish, clutching the phone in a hand that's shaking, and try to stay calm in spite of the tornado of panic sweeping over me.

Trish's eyes are wide with alarm. She listens to Mrs. Gerard, responds in French, listens some more.

I don't catch all the French, but I know she told Mrs. Gerard about the message she got on her cell. The rest is clear when Trish slowly lowers the phone and meets our eyes.

"Cecily's missing," she whispers.

FIVE

TRISH SITS BETWEEN US ON THE COUCH. "MRS.
Gerard said she let Cecily off at a corner bakery near the
school. So she could get a croissant—she'd missed school
lunch. She was supposed to eat, then go to class."

Trish's voice trembles as she continues, "Mrs. Gerard got a
text message from Cecily at two, saying she was coming home
with me to study lines for the play. She was supposed to call
her mother to come pick her up when we were finished."

A wave of nausea hits me like a gut punch. Whatever
happened, it had been carefully orchestrated to make sure
Cecily wouldn't be missed until early evening. If this were any
other kid in any other place, what happened might be viewed
by the police as a simple case of a teen-ager running away.

But in this particular time and place, I'm afraid there's
little doubt that Cecily in another kidnapping victim.

"What else did she say, honey?" I ask gently.

Trish was trying hard not to cry. "That she was going to
call the police. She's afraid Cecily—"

She can't finish the sentence, her words strangling in her throat.

I'm close to tears, too. But mine are tears of anger. My first thought is that *I* know who to call. This may not be the Marseille thing that Vlad referred to at the cottage, but he's going to help me find Trish's friend. I'll make sure of it. He has connections on both sides of the law.

I won't let Trish lose someone else.

———●●●———

Vlad agrees to come to the house in the morning. He doesn't let on if the kidnappings had anything to do with his own concerns and he doesn't argue that it's not vampire business, but says he'll look into it for me.

By the time I'm off the phone with Vlad, the police are at our door. Dad leads them into the living room.

The officers who come to take Trish's statement are both middle-aged males, paunchy, with faces marked by the weight of the tragedy they've come to investigate. They speak in French too fast for me to understand. Trish and Dad have no trouble, though, and I watch as they ping-pong back and forth—asking and answering questions. If I had any doubts before, the expressions on the officers' faces confirm that they fear Cecily is the latest victim in the string of kidnappings.

As they talk, I try to remember what I read about the crimes. The parents all got ransom demands, paid them, but the girls were killed anyway. How much time transpired between the ransom calls and the discovery of the bodies?

Three days, I think, before the bodies were found in Northern Marseille.

The police finish their inquiry and Dad shows them out. "You look worn out," he says to Trish. "Why don't you go on up to bed. If we hear anything, we'll wake you."

She looks like she's going to object. She also looks bone-weary. "Go on, Trish," I add. "Even if you can't sleep, just lie down."

But she shakes her head. "I want to be right here if there's any news."

"Okay." I take an afghan from the back of the couch. "Then at least wrap up and stretch out on the couch. How's that?"

She takes the afghan from my hands. "Okay. But I won't sleep."

"Just rest." I tuck her in, plumping a pillow beneath her head. "Dad and I will be in the kitchen if you need us."

She nods wearily. Dad leans over to kiss her cheek. "We're right here, sweetie-pie."

He follows me into the kitchen. I pull the pocket door closed behind us before asking, "What did the police say?"

He crosses to the counter, busying himself with setting up the coffee maker. "Cecily's disappearance fits the profile of the other abductions. All the girls were taken on their way to school. All had text messages sent from their cell phones to family and friends giving the kidnappers hours to spirit them away before anyone realized they were missing."

He's not looking at me while he speaks. When the coffee maker starts to perk, he reaches up to pull mugs from a cabinet. One of the mugs slips from his grasp. I catch it before it hits the floor.

Thank you, vampire reflexes.

But Dad is so upset, he doesn't even comment on the fact that I just performed a super-human feat. Calmly, I take the mugs from him. "We'll keep Trish safe," I say gently.

He finally meets my eyes. "I keep thinking it could have been Trish today."

I lead him to the table and gently guide him into a chair. I know that's not all he's thinking. It's only been three weeks since Mom died. I blow out a breath and ask, "Did they happen to say how they think Cecily was targeted?" I take the chair beside him.

He nods. "Yes. In fact, they thought the fact that she was on television last night got the kidnapper's attention. The reporters not only told them what school she went to, but that she'd be arriving late today. It was a perfect set up."

The coffee maker chimes. I pour two cups and bring them back to the table. "I have a friend coming tomorrow morning," I tell Dad. "He came to our wedding so you might remember him. His name is Vlad and he has a lot of connections that could be useful. He's going to help us find Cecily."

"You think he can do anything the police can't?"

I choose my words carefully. "He's been around a long time. He knows Marseille better than anyone. I trust him with my life. Even more, I'd trust him with Trish's."

Dad takes my hand. "I don't think Trish could stand it if anything happened to her friend. Not so soon after—"

I don't let him finish. I squeeze his hand. "We'll find Cecily. We'll get her back."

He releases a breath. "We have to."

———●●●———

We keep Trish home from school, as much for our sake as hers. She doesn't argue. When Dad calls the school to let them know, he's informed that as many as half the students are out. News of Cecily's abduction made the front page of every newspaper.

Dad gave instructions to the work crew and sent them to the fields without him. He, Trish, and I have a silent breakfast. We are each wrapped up in our own thoughts.

At eight, we get a call from Mrs. Gerard. They were contacted by telephone and a ransom demand made. Trish puts the call on speaker so Dad and I can hear.

Mrs. Gerard's voice is heavy with fatigue, but she methodically relates the facts in halting English. "The kidnappers used a burner phone," she says, "And while the police were able to ascertain where the call was made from, an industrial area in Marseille, it will take days or weeks to trace it back to a purchaser." She pauses, draws a heavy breath, continues. "The kidnappers are asking two hundred-fifty thousand Euros to be dropped tomorrow morning at a location they'll name then. We're arranging for the money to be delivered to us this afternoon by courier."

She switches to French to say a few more words to Trish before hanging up.

I look from Trish to Dad. We're all thinking it—if they follow the same time table as before, Cecily has two days to live.

———————————•••———————————

Vlad is at the door at nine sharp.

Trish and Dad recognize him from the wedding at once. A man with his distinctive look isn't easily forgotten. I can't remember how I introduced him, I'm sure it wasn't Vlad Dracul, former Prince of Wallachian. Or Vlad the Impaler. But I needn't have worried. Dad is only concerned with one thing.

"Anna tells us you might be able to help find Trish's friend." He shakes Vlad's hand. "If you do, we will be forever in your debt."

Vlad gives me a surreptitious wink. *Forever* is a strong word to use with a vampire. To my dad, he says, "I have put out feelers. I'm confident I will hear something this morning." He looks over at Trish. "We will find your friend."

Dad offers him a cup of coffee, which he accepts. He asks Dad about grape prospects for the year and they enter into a discussion of soil content and moisture levels. I can tell Dad is impressed with his knowledge of wine making. I suppose it's only one of hundreds of subjects Vlad is conversant in. After all, he's been living in this area for centuries.

Trish and I leave them and walk out into the garden. She's trying to be brave, but the stress of waiting shows on her face.

I don't try to distract her with empty slogans about positive thinking. It never worked for me.

We take seats around a big wooden table under a sprawling ancient oak. My mother used to call this our outdoor dining room. The tree hasn't completely leafed out yet, but its promise of shelter from a hot summer sun is already evident.

Trish cups her hands around her coffee mug. "Do you think your friend can really find Cecily?"

Her tone is hesitant, hopeful.

"Yes." My tone is confident, positive.

"Why?" She raises her eyes to meet mine. "What can he do that the police haven't been able to?"

I wonder how I should answer that question. Trish knows nothing of vampires in general, let alone that her aunt is one. Or that Vlad is one of the oldest vampires in existence and, like Moriarty in the Sherlock Holmes tales, has a web of informants that span not only France, but Europe and beyond.

"He's not like the rest of us, is he?" she asks when it's clear I'm floundering.

I release a breath. "How do you mean?"

"I'm not sure. He looks young—well, younger than Granddad, I mean. But his eyes. They're old." She shakes her head. "I'm not explaining it very well."

Ah, but you are. A vampire's eyes are indeed the windows of his soul, and reflected in Vlad's are centuries of life. Centuries of making mistakes and trying to rectify them.

Finding Cecily safe will be another of those acts of restitution on Vlad's part to help balance the scales.

Trish's eyes are on me, I feel her gaze like a ray of warm sunlight. She's waiting for me to say something. I take a deep breath.

"You're right in some respects," I begin. "Vlad is different in that he has steeped himself in history. He lives as much in at the past as he does in the present. But he travels in different worlds—those of the just and unjust. If there is an organization behind these abductions, he'll find it."

"But he hasn't before this." Her tone is belligerent, accusatory. "Why didn't he try to find the kidnappers when the first three girls were killed? He waits until he's *asked* to get involved? He didn't care about the others?"

She's shuddering, angry color flooding her face.

I move around the table to console her—I can't think of anything else to do—and run into Vlad as he joins us from the house. I have been so absorbed with Trish's pain, I didn't sense his approach. His expression says he heard Trish, and there is sorrow in his eyes.

He stands beside her. "I should have gotten involved earlier," he says. "I regret that. Your aunt said I live as much in the past as I do in the present. She's right. I tend to cocoon myself away with my books and manuscripts. Sometimes months go by before I surface. If it wasn't for your aunt, this deplorable situation might have gone on for God only knows how long and I would have known nothing about it. But I'm here now. And I just got a promising lead. Your aunt and I will pursue it and if all goes well, we will have your friend back with her family before the day's end."

Trish jumps to her feet. "I want to go with you."

Vlad answers before I can. "No. You need to stay here with your grandfather. Where we are going is no place for—"

"For a what?" Trish snaps. "For a child? I am not a child."

Vlad smiles. "No. You are not a child. And that is not what I was going to say. It will be dangerous. Your aunt is trained to deal with the kind of characters we will encounter. You are not. We promise, you will be the first to hear when we get Cecily to safety. Then you and your grandfather can be with her parents when we bring her back."

"How can you be so sure you will find her?" Trish asks pointedly.

"You have to trust me."

Dad strides down the path from the house. He has one of my jackets in one hand and my cell phone in the other. "Vlad said this would be all you need." He hands me the phone and the jacket. "Are you ready to go?"

I shrug into the jacket, slip the phone into an inside pocket. We exchange a wordless hug, then I turn to Trish.

"We'll call as soon as we have news."

Trish puts both arms around me and squeezes. "Be safe, Aunt Anna," she says. "Bring Cecily back but be safe."

I kiss the top of her head and gently extricate myself. Vlad nods to me, to my grandfather and Trish. "I'll bring them both back," he says.

We leave two of the people I love most in the world standing close together under that big oak.

SIX

I'M SURPRISED TO SEE IT ISN'T VLAD'S DUCATI waiting for us in the driveway. It's a van.

A white, side-door, mini-van.

It's so unexpected, I stop and stare.

"You're driving *that?*"

He stops, too, and raises an eyebrow. "What's wrong with it?"

"Nothing. Only you're about as far from the image of a soccer-mom as I am from a nun."

I open the passenger side door and hoist myself in. The inside is clean but littered with toys. I pick up a stuffed bear and toss it into the back.

He takes his place behind the wheel. "What's a soccer-mom?"

I roll my eyes. He starts the van and turns it around so we're heading for the road. "Where are we going?"

"Ever heard of Niaux?"

"No. Where is it?"

"About three hours from here."

I stare again. "We could run it in one."

"We could," he replies. "But how do you propose we bring Cecily back?"

"Good point." I release a breath. "I hope you're right about bringing Cecily back. I couldn't bear to disappoint Trish."

"We won't."

"And you're so sure, why?"

We're heading for the highway. "Because I know who's behind the kidnappings and why they're doing it."

He's making me pull information out of him in bits and pieces and my patience finally runs out. "Look, Vlad—enough. Tell me where we're going and who we're dealing with."

He grimaces. "It's unpleasant," he says. "So what would you like to know first? Where we're going? Why the girls were kidnapped? Or who is behind the plot?"

I settle back in the seat. We're in for a long drive. I ponder the question for a moment before replying, "How about who?"

He nods. "First, a little background. You've no doubt heard about the unrest in Marseille. There is a growing faction in the government that wants to keep France for the French. They want to curtail immigration and drive foreigners back to their own countries. It's becoming almost an obsession for some. And they're winning the hearts and minds of a great many Frenchmen."

I stir in my seat. "Sounds uncomfortably like something that happened here in Europe in the thirties."

"It could head just that way. Cooler heads prevail for the present. But Marseille is a huge city with a large immigrant population, widespread poverty and one of the highest unemployment rates in the country. The police played up the fact that the kidnappers were immigrant gangs from *les banlieue défavorisée*. Even hinted that there might be a Muslim connection. And if the girls had been let go uninjured after the exchange of money, not much might have been made of it save a growing unrest toward foreigners. But such has not been the case."

"Why is that, do you think?"

He turns serious dark eyes to me. "It is very disturbing. What my contacts tell me makes me fear for France. The word is that the local government is behind what's happening. That they orchestrated the kidnappings—or at least turned a blind eye to them—not foreseeing that the *gangs* they encouraged would kill their victims. They wanted to make it so uncomfortable for immigrants that they would leave Marseille and the unrest would spread from there to all of France."

Disturbing doesn't begin to describe the emotions welling up in me. "The *government* is behind what's happening here?" My voice rises. "What kind of country is this?"

Vlad clucks his tongue and shoots me an ironic smile. "You think your own country is unsusceptible to thinking of this sort? Look at your history, Anna."

I raise an eyebrow and irritably wave a hand for him to go on.

After a moment, he continues. "Nevertheless, it does get worse. My contact tells me that there are no immigrant gangs involved at all. That the police themselves are perpetrating these crimes. Not all of the police, of course, and the identities of the murderers are a closely guarded secret. But when the parents of the girls began paying the ransoms, and the policemen saw how much easy money was to be made…. Well, they decided to change the game."

"But why kill the girls?" I ask, still trying to wrap my head around the idea that policemen were involved.

"Most likely because the girls could identify them," he answers. "Or at the very least, confirm that their kidnappers were native Frenchmen."

I let this sink in a moment. I know there are dirty cops. That's not a surprise. But what is a surprise, is that cops would go as far as to kill innocent young girls to protect their own identity. "Who came up with this brilliant scheme?" I ask, fighting a sudden urge to find those responsible and tear their throats out.

Vlad reads the emotion boiling in me. "I doubt we'll get the chance to meet the leader," he says. "I understand he's on vacation somewhere in the Mediterranean. Distancing himself from the fallout now that the plan has gone so wrong."

"So why are we headed for Niaux?"

"Niaux is located in the foothills of the Pyrenees. There is a cave there where prehistoric paintings have been discovered. It's quite a popular tourist attraction. That's where the kidnappers have been taking their victims."

"To a tourist attraction?"

"Nearby. And when you think of it, it's quite a smart plan. Niaux is far enough from Marseille to be eliminated in any area search for the girls. No one would think to look so far from the abduction sites."

"And all the girls' families were unaware that their daughters were missing," I add quickly, "because the kidnappers were careful to leave text messages explaining their absences. It gave them plenty of time to get the girls out of the area."

Vlad nods. "Then, when the girls are killed, their bodies are taken back and dumped near Marseille. Adding to the suspicion that immigrants are involved."

We travel in silence for some time. The countryside is beautiful—layered in shades of green only springtime can produce. How can such a lovely country produce such monsters? Men willing to kill, then blame it on an innocent population who wants only to achieve a better life for themselves and their families.

I have to admit, though, it's an old story.

"Are you going to tell me who your snitch was?" I ask finally.

"Snitch?"

"Informant."

"Ah. No. It's better no one knows."

But my instincts tell me I can figure it out. "It's one of the kidnappers, isn't it? Someone whose conscience finally got the better of him."

That elicits a snicker. "Conscience? No. Something much more appealing to one such as he. I offered a huge reward for information. Circulated the information through my underbelly—"

"Underworld," I correct.

"*Underworld* contacts. It worked."

"I take it he won't be among those we find with Cecily today," I say wryly.

"No. Today he is elsewhere."

"Lucky for him."

SEVEN

THE ROAD WINDS UPWARD NOW, THROUGH gently rolling, glacier-carved hills. I find myself wondering about Vlad. How easy it was for him to find out where Cecily was and how in one day, we will close down this kidnapping operation.

But not before three girls were killed.

"Were you serious about what you told Trish? Were you really so self-absorbed that you were unaware that three young girls had been kidnapped and murdered?"

The look Vlad sends me is scathing. The heat of his sudden anger sends a scorching bolt through me. "Are there not murders of innocents taking place in *your* country everyday? Do you involve yourself in them? I read the newspapers. There are serial killers at work in every state of your union. What are you doing about them?"

Heat floods my face. He's right. I have no right to criticize him. He's involved now because I asked him to be. What sends a chill through me is that if I hadn't been here to ask, what would have happened to Trish's friend?

Vlad reads my thoughts and his temper cools. *Perhaps it has been too long since I've had close human connections,* he says. *I forgot how personal this is to you.*

Still, I should not have called you self-absorbed. It's not something one friend says to another.

Vlad relaxes and his thoughts turn to how we'll approach the cave where Cecily is being held.

"Cave?" I repeat aloud.

"We are going to a valley where the Niaux Cave is located. Prehistoric paintings were discovered there. On the other side of the valley, is another cave. It's thought that in this cave, the ancient artists who left the paintings lived with their families. This cave is harder to get to and not open to the public. It's also sheltered so one could hide a person inside and they would not be exposed to the elements."

"How will we approach it?"

"The cave has a low-ceilinged entrance that opens to a wide cavern. There is no way to approach from the front without being seen. To the back of the cavern, however, there is another entrance angled down through rock. It's narrow, but we should have no trouble navigating it. My informant said they leave two people with the girl at all times. Once inside, between us we should have no trouble subduing two humans."

"I hope they put up a fight," I mumble, fingers flexing in anticipation.

Vlad shakes his head. "Remember, Anna, Cecily will be there. We can't damage the humans too much. How will we explain it?"

He's right, at some point, we'll have to bring in the police. "Did you have a plan for turning these scumbags in?"

"At my call, my informant will notify the local police in Niaux of strange goings-on in the cave. When they arrive, our story will be that we are spelunkers who happened upon the girl and her kidnappers. We were able to surprise them and free the girl. At that point, we are out of it and the locals take over."

"So I won't be able to take even a little blood?" I whine.

He clucks his tongue. "Trebuie doar mâncat, Anna, nu fi un pic porc."

I've never heard him speak his native language before. I raise a questioning eyebrow. "Do I want to know what that means?"

"You just ate, Anna," he says, "Don't be a *petit cochon*."

Cochon? *Tha*t I understand.

We're scrambling up a rocky hillside. Vlad's feet hardly touch the ground. It's not so easy for me, but I have no trouble keeping up. We reach what looks like chimney in the rock. Vlad signals that this is our entry point. There are two backpacks on the ground as well as a coil of rope.

I reach down and hoist one of the backpacks. "Your informant?"

"We need to make our story plausible." He shrugs into the second backpack and picks up the rope.

I peer down inside the hole. Inky darkness at first. Then vampire vision kicks in. It's a steep drop, but the walls are narrow enough that I know I can lever myself down. I give Vlad a thumbs-up and shimmy inside.

Silently, I chimney toward the bottom. The rocks bite into my palms. I hear voices from below—far away voices so I know they won't see us until we want them to.

My feet touch the floor of the cave. I step aside and Vlad floats noiselessly down to stand beside me.

"Why didn't I think of that?" I whisper, rubbing bruised palms.

We make our way toward the voices. The cave is huge, high-ceilinged so we can walk upright, with a surprisingly flat floor. Here and there, we see remnants of the civilization that occupied this space. Fire pits and grooved mortars. It's warm, not damp and cold as one would expect.

The voices grow louder.

And another sound.

Quiet sobbing.

It makes the blood lust flare. Blood lust for the animals who would do this to a child.

Vlad puts his hand on my arm and shakes his head. *Keep it together, Anna.*

I draw a deep breath, release it slowly. He nods when he feels I've regained composure and starts ahead.

The path bends before us. We sense rather than see that the men are on the other side. Vlad puts a finger to his lips. *I'll go in first. After the men. You go to the girl.*

I nod.

Vlad moves so fast, he's a shadow on the wall of the cave. The vampire takes over and I'm on his heels, seeking out Cecily in the dim light. She's bound hand and foot, a torn blanket thrown over her. I gather her up, tear off the ropes binding her and strip off the dirty cloth covering her mouth. "Stay here," I whisper, my voice a hoarse whisper.

I turn to the sounds of a scuffle.

But the battle—such as it was—is over. Two men lie on their backs, mouths gaping open, breath coming in shallow gasps. Vlad has taken their guns and flung them into the recesses of the cave. His eyes glow like a cat's in the flickering light of a campfire.

"How's the girl?" he asks me.

Cecily has staggered to her feet. She looks at Vlad, his vampire cat-like eyes still burning. Then she looks at me. "What are you?" she asks, fear reasserting itself. Her English is halting and broken.

Vlad pulls out his phone. "I'll have to make the call from outside," he says to me. "Will you be alright?"

I nod. I can't do anything about my eyes, they will return to normal as soon as vampire retreats, but I try to modulate my voice to alleviate her fear.

"I'm Trish's Aunt Anna," I say. "My friend and I have come to take you home."

"But your eyes—" She takes a step back. "What's wrong with them?"

"Oh that. I'm wearing special contact lenses. They help me see in the dark. Spelunker gear."

"Spelunker?" she repeats.

I pull the backpack off. "You know, people who investigate caves."

"Is that how you found me?"

She doesn't wait for an answer. She throws her arms around my neck. "Thank you. Thank you."

I hug her back, grinning. "*Pas de quoi!*."

When the Naiux police arrive, I let Vlad do all the talking. In French, he tells them of our "cave explorations" and how we happened upon the girl and her abductors. I hear much excited chatter among the constables. Cecily is carefully examined and questioned before a call to her mother confirms to the police that we have permission to bring her home. The kidnappers are bundled not-to-gently off to jail.

Cecily keeps looking at Vlad and me. Our human personas are back and I can tell she's wondering about the "contact lenses." She doesn't ask, though, and I don't mention them again.

The mood on the drive home is far lighter than the mood on the way to Naiux. Cecily tries to keep up a conversation, but within a few minutes, her head begins to nod.

"Stretch out," I tell her. "We have a long drive and they'll be a lot of excited people waiting for you at home. Sleep while you can."

She doesn't argue. There is a blanket among the kids' toys in the back. She lays herself down across the seat, pulls the blanket up around her shoulders.

I reach behind the seat and tuck her in. Within seconds, she's asleep.

Poor kid, I say to Vlad. *She must be exhausted.*

She has a lot to be thankful for, he comments. *She owes you her life, you know.*

She owes you *her life,* I correct. *You made the calls that solved the mystery. I was along for the ride.*

Let us just say that we *make a good team.*

I let a moment pass, wondering if I should bring up the subject. Too late I realize Vlad is in my head. He slips in so unobtrusively that when he speaks, I jump.

You want to know what I was talking about with Amélie and Alexander. It's not a question.

I thought it might have something to do with this, I reply, gesturing to the back seat. *Now, I suspect not. Perhaps I could be of help.*

He never takes his eyes from the road, but I feel his gaze like the warmth from a fire. He has abilities far beyond those of the normal vampire—certainly beyond mine. I don't try to intrude on his thoughts. It's his decision and as much as I would love to be taken into his confidence, I won't push.

Another long moment goes by. He heaves a sigh. *It's Steffan's band of toadies. Back to cause trouble.*

I'm startled into silence. I can't believe they would have dared come back. Vlad threatened them with the same fate as their leader, Steffan—immediate beheading.

But it's more than that. Vlad granted the six vampires clemency because of me. Because I asked it of him.

What are they threatening? I ask, knowing Vlad is privy to all I'm thinking and feeling.

The same as Steffan. A take-over of the mortal world. Only now they've recruited even more followers. And when the story breaks of how French police were behind the kidnappings, they'll point to that as proof that mortals are base animals, unworthy to rule themselves. They'll want to put their plan into action.

Is it the same plan as before? To introduce vampires into all aspects of government?

A slow but sure takeover.

A niggling seed of guilt starts to sprout thorns. If I hadn't asked Vlad for help, maybe the vampires wouldn't have the kidnappings to use as a rallying cry. Maybe the police themselves would have rooted out their guilty cohorts.

But maybe Cecily would have been killed before that happened.

Don't try to second guess, Vlad says, in my head again. *If it hadn't been this, it would have been something else. Humans give us plenty of reasons to condemn their actions.*

I press the palms of my hands against my eyes, weary of the way mortals and immortals are constantly at war, either with each other or themselves. Nothing I can do about that. But there's one thing I'm sure of. I straighten and turn to Vlad. *What can I do to help?*

EIGHT

FOR ONCE, VLAD DOESN'T GIVE ME A LECTURE about how I have no standing here or how what's happening is none of my business. Rather, he casts a sideways glance at me and for a moment, I see reflected in his eyes the uncomfortable confirmation that he acknowledges I *did* have something to do with the predicament he finds himself in.

I swallow and nod. *Go on.*

I am to meet with a representative of Vampires for Dominion. He again glances my way. *It's what they call themselves. I am certain at that meeting an assassination attempt on my life will be made. The meeting is to be at a time and place of my choosing. I am to come alone, as is this representative.*

You don't trust them?

I'd be a fool to. No matter where I pick, if a determined vampire sets out to kill me, I am most probably dead.

Not if you have a determined vampire of your own to prevent it. I close my eyes a moment, pondering the situation. *What if you meet on my father's estate? There's an old wine press in an isolated corner of the vineyard. It's built of stone, small windows, only one door.*

That would certainly prevent someone from ambushing us, Vlad says. *Except on the way in or out.*

I've thought of that, too. Excitement starts to bubble as a plan takes form. *You trust Amélie and Alexander. Are there more vampires in your court?*

Yes, although few I trust as I trust Amélie and Alexander." He nods in my direction. *Or you.*

Then the three of us will be your back-up. When are you contacting these Vampires for Dominion?

This evening. I'm to name the time and place.

Set the meeting for tomorrow-midnight. Tomorrow morning, we'll go meet with Amélie and Alexander and make a plan. In the meantime, I'll reconnoiter the old wine press building. It's been awhile since I've been out there, but I think there's just one overgrown path that leads to it.

You almost sound excited, Vlad comments wryly.

I have a horse in this race, too, you know. My father and niece live here. I realize if this faction is successful, nothing may change in their lifetimes. Still, it would be a dangerous precedent to allow.

I let my voice drop, remembering what Steffan and his followers wanted to do. Their plan was to slowly and progressively replace human politicians with vampires until vampires controlled the government. It might take a generation or two, but what is that to an immortal? Once the plan succeeded, vampires would out themselves. Humans would be relegated to a servant class whose primary functions would be to serve as a food source or work force.

It was a good plan that would have been put into play had not Vlad found out about it. The leader, Steffan, was put to the final death—or so we thought. But he had a back-up plan that involved him jumping into another body at the fatal moment. It took Vlad, Frey and I to track him down and destroy him. This time for good.

But I encouraged Vlad to show mercy to Steffan's six lieutenants. I never dreamed they'd return from exile—especially so soon.

You can't blame yourself for being merciful, Vlad says, once again knowing exactly what I'm thinking and feeling. *I was caught by surprise myself.*

How does Marseille figure in this? I ask.

It's where they're hiding. In the same Banelieu as the immigrants who were to be blamed for the kidnappings. It is one of the poorest in France and the least policed. They can feed with impunity since it is a place that is considered outside the law.

Cecily stirs in the back seat, stretches, and sits up. "How much longer?" she asks.

Vlad holds up a hand. "Five minutes."

She smoothes her clothes. "Anna, have you a *brosse à cheveux?*

But I have nothing with me but a jacket and a cell phone.

"Look in the glove box," Vlad says.

I do—there's a comb and some wet wipes. "Here," I hand them back to her. "These will help."

She busies herself tidying up.

I smile at Vlad. *You are quite the Boy Scout.*

He smiles back. *Ah, that reference I know. Always prepared.*

NINE

WE'D CALLED AHEAD TO LET CECILY'S FAMILY
know we would be arriving shortly. Vlad was given her ad-
dress by the police in Niaux and navigates the streets outside
Lorgues with practiced efficiency.

As soon as we pull into the driveway, the front door flies
open. Cecily's parents, a young man whom I assume to be
a brother, Trish and Dad rush out to meet us. Two policemen stand back, allowing the reunion to take place without
interference. I'm sure they have many questions for Cecily.
Especially since her kidnappers were two of their own.

I look at them with some suspicion. *How do we know they
weren't part of the plot?* I ask Vlad.

We don't, he replies. *Only when the two we caught are re-
turned and questioned will we know. And even then, they may
refuse to name accomplices. They are most probably family men
themselves and fearful of retaliation. But their plot will he re-
vealed. I believe it's over.*

Cecily and Trish are hugging and crying. The Gerards crowd Vlad and I, their exuberant outpouring of gratitude manifesting itself in an explosion of French I can't keep up with.

The meaning is clear, though, even though I don't understand every word. I accept their thanks and quietly slip away to join Dad on the porch steps.

He hugs me. "You did good, kid," he says.

Cecily's mom begins shepherding everyone up the stairs and into the house. "Venez. Il est la nourriture et le vin à l'intérieur. Nous allons manger."

I glance over at Vlad. Neither of us want to go through the charade of eating.

He offers us an out. "Merci, Mme Gérard. Mais je dois retourner la fourgonnette maintenant et Anna et je ai un rendez-vous avec le chef de police de la ville."

Dad whispers the translation, recognizing that I caught only a few words. Something about returning the van and an appointment with the Lorgues Chief of Police.

"You go, honey," he says. "I'll stay. Trish and I will see you at home later."

The Gerards are just as gracious in bidding us goodbye. Cecily approaches with Trish.

"I don't know how to thank you," she says. There is no suspicion or timidity in her voice. She hugs us one at a time. Trish, her eyes brimming with tears, whispers over her head. "Thank you, Aunt Anna."

I hug my niece, and watch as the two stroll arm in arm into the house.

We did good, indeed.

Vlad backs the van out of the driveway.

"I should have known this wasn't your van," I say. "Definitely not your style."

He laughs. "It belongs to a friend of mine." He shoots me a sly smile. "A soccer-mom."

I grin back. "I was right. What about the other? Do we really have an appointment with the Chief of Police?"

"Well, that part wasn't exactly true," he concedes. "I'm sure we'll be hearing from the authorities before the case goes to trial, but not this afternoon."

The "soccer mom" turns out to be human, an attractive thirty-something living on the edge of Lourges. I can tell by her demeanor with Vlad that they are more than just friends. I wonder if she is a host but her polite friendliness to me gives nothing away. We leave on Vlad's Ducati.

After he whispers something in her ear that makes the color rise in her cheeks.

"Heavy date?" I ask when we've pulled away.

He shrugs. "I owe her for the use of the van. I told her I'd be back tonight to pay."

His thoughts reflect the method of payment he has in mind until I forcefully shut them down. He chuckles.

Vlad drops me off at the estate with the promise to call in the morning after he talks with Amélie and Alexander. I wave him off and go inside.

The house is quiet without Dad and Trish. I grab a bottle of water from the fridge and head out to check the old wine press. It takes me awhile to find the path, but once I do, it's easy going.

I pass workers in the vineyards on my way. They look up as I go, some raise a hand in greeting. I know immigrant workers are a political hot potato in many countries, but France seems to have a dangerously radical faction who thinks blaming them for the murder of innocent children is an acceptable solution.

The press is in an old stone building, probably hundreds of years old. It is as tall as a two story building, but the windows on three sides are all about five feet from the ground and narrow slits that would allow little light inside. The door is an opening, nothing more, with a ragged leather curtain hung from wooden pegs. I push it aside and go in.

It smells mainly of dirt and decay. The press itself has long gone to ruin, only rotted timbers piled in the center remain. The wood is stained purple and there is the lingering odor of fruit to remind one of the decades of grape pressing that went on here. Puffs of dust rise from my footfalls. I think it's a possibility that no one has been in here since the original owner, another vampire—my maker, in fact, tred these floors.

The thought sends a shiver down my spine. Avery was an evil bastard who fooled me not once, but twice.

He's gone now. Of that, I'm certain.

I shake away the gloom and walk back outside.

I was right in offering this place to Vlad. There is only one way in and one way out. In the dark, it won't be easy to conceal myself in a field not yet budded. But my eyes go to the roof. I scale the walls with ease. It is flat up here with a six inch parapet behind which three vampires can easily conceal themselves. People looking for an ambush usually look everywhere but up. Plus, there is a pipe that extends down into the building, maybe to allow fresh air inside, I'm not sure. But it would make listening to what's going on inside effortless—especially for a vampire.

I go back to the house to await the return of my father and Trish. But the celebration at the Gerards must go on until well past midnight and I'm fast asleep by then.

TEN

THE MOOD AT BREAKFAST IS CELEBRATORY.
Trish, even after not getting a great deal of sleep last night (I heard them come in at one in the morning)is beaming. She eats a hearty breakfast, thanking me again and again until I shoo her off to the school bus. It is such a relief to have things back to normal.

My dad goes off to the vineyards and I'm left to await Vlad's call. Instead of that, though, he appears in the driveway, the Ducati announcing his arrival as surely as if he had blown an airhorn. I greet him with coffee, which he takes with an appreciative smile.

"This is early for you, isn't it?" I ask.

"Good God, yes," he replies. "But since it may be my last day on this earth, I decided not to waste a moment of it." He takes a sip and rolls his eyes. "Heaven. Speaking of which, how is Trish?"

But I'm caught off guard by his first remark. "I thought it was to be a one-on-one meeting?"

He shrugs. "My informants tell me there is talk of an ambush."

"But you suspected as much. Are you really afraid of these vampires?"

He lifts a shoulder noncommittally. "I don't want to underestimate them. They are firm in their resolve to have their way and resentful that I killed their leader in such a public way."

"You sound resigned. I don't know if I like that."

Vlad waves a hand. "You know how long I have lived. Maybe it's time to pass the torch."

His remarks send a shudder through me. "What are you saying? Who could possibly take your place?"

He looks at me over the rim of his coffee cup as he drinks and says nothing.

The silence, however, speaks volumes.

My temper flares. "You can't be serious. What happened to *you have no say in what happens here, Anna?* Or, *remember you have no power here.* The European vampires don't even recognize me as the Chosen One. How do you think they'd respond to you making me their leader?"

"They wouldn't have a choice, would they?"

"Well, I do," I snap quickly. "And the answer is no. Once I go back to the states, I have no idea what I'll be dealing with there. I'm not about to take on anything else."

Vlad raises his eyebrows but doesn't respond.

Again.

I rage on, "If you're intent on stepping down, what about naming Amélie and Alexander your successors as you did Steffan? They are strong vampires, loyal to you." I take a step closer. "And anyway, nothing is going to happen to you tonight. I have a plan. One or six vampires, it will make no difference. Did you call Amélie and Alexander?"

Vlad has finished his coffee. He hands the mug back to me. "Yes. They are willing to help."

"Then let's take a walk. I'll show you what I have in mind."

Vlad and I start out across the vineyards to the old press. I show him the building and demonstrate how easily we can conceal ourselves on the roof, all the while listening to what goes on inside. "If there's any hint of ambush, we can be inside before Steffan's toadies know what hit them. Four against six are certainly better odds than one against six."

"You are very sure of yourself," Vlad remarks.

"And you very unsure." I take his arm. "What is it? This is so unlike you."

He leans against the parapet and gazes out at the vineyards. "What happened to Trish's friend made me aware of a fact I've long avoided. I have no interest in what happens to humans around me, even when innocents are murdered in my own back yard. I know I accused you of doing the same thing, but I also know you've put your life on the line for those humans you love again and again. No one can save the world. But we should be willing to save the little corner we occupy. You do."

"And you can, too. You proved it. Now all you need do is not cloister yourself so. Stepping down or getting yourself killed is not an answer. Shutting down the fanatics that think mortals have no purpose save to be blood bags or servants is."

Vlad doesn't speak for a long moment. He's shut me out of his thoughts effectively leaving me alone with mine. Have I said too much or too little?

After several moments, Vlad straightens. "You know, there is another alternative," he says.

"To what?"

He keeps his gaze focused on the horizon. "You and I could rule together."

His answer takes me so by surprise, I gasp, "I don't understand." But even as I say the words, I know it's untrue. I understand very well.

Vlad knows it, too.

He turns and takes my chin, tilting my face toward him. "From the moment, I saw you I knew. Since my wife centuries ago, you are the first woman whom I could love as an equal."

I twist away. "You also know that's impossible."

"Because of Frey?" Vlad spits his name like a curse.

His venom is as unexpected as it is cruel. "I owe you for saving Trish's friend," I say slowly. "I owe you for helping me in the dark time with my mother. I owe you for allowing me to live in your country as a vampire. I am willing to repay you with this—" I wave my hand around. "But I do not owe you my heart."

His eyes bore into mine before he breaks the spell and looks away. "I don't apologize for speaking my mind," he says.

"As I don't apologize for speaking mine," I reply.

He nods. "We should go to Amélie's. That is, if you still wish to help me."

"I wish to help your community," I say. "Both human and vampire."

He doesn't look at me as we depart. I have the feeling he may never look at me again.

ELEVEN

I DRIVE MY OWN CAR TO AMÉLIE AND ALEXAN-
der's. It makes the most sense since Vlad needs to be at home
for the car that will bring him to the meeting. He and the
leader of the conspiracy, a vampire named Renaldo, would
come together. Presumably as an effort to thwart an attack.
Vlad would choose the driver.

As I follow the Ducati into the countryside, I keep re-
playing the scene between Vlad and I on the roof. Everything
about him this morning was odd. From his apparent resigna-
tion to being killed to his wanting to give up his position as
vampire ruler to his abrupt proposal that we rule together. For
the first time since we met, he was a stranger.

The vampire couple is waiting for us. Amélie greets me
like an old friend, introducing Alexander as he had been in his
study when I came to feed. He is not at all what I expected—
portly where Amélie is thin, with the bearing of a jolly monk,
a face open and friendly, a head balding on top, a mouth made
for laughter. His eyes twinkle when he takes my hand.

I see why Vlad is so taken with you, he says.

He means it as a compliment but it makes me uneasy. What has Vlad been telling them?

Amélie senses my apprehension. *Enough, my love,* she says. *You are embarrassing Anna. And I told you, she is a very happily married woman.*

Alexander raises an eyebrow but doesn't reply. He looks at Vlad who shifts nervously and refuses to meet his eyes.

Once again, Amélie breaks the uneasy silence. *Anna, Vlad tells us you have a plan for tonight. It's important that we rid ourselves of these dissenters once and for all. This evening, when they are all together, may be the only chance to strike that blow.*

Her words catch me unawares. *You misunderstand. I was under the impression we were going to act only if there was an attack on Vlad.*

Puzzled glances between husband and wife make me realize I was the one who misunderstood. Or who was led to misunderstand.

Vlad and I must talk, I say. *Will you excuse us?*

I lead Vlad outside. Anger bubbles like a hot springs inside me, threatening to erupt. I swallow it back, hard, and temper my voice when I can trust myself to speak.

You are planning to kill the dissenters tonight?

Do you not think they deserve to die? I told them what would happen if they came back to the continent. And brazenly, they disobeyed.

His tone is that of ruler once again. Abrupt, decisive.

Why have you brought me into this? I ask. *You have many loyal followers who would have gladly help you vanquish these vampires.*

Did you not supplicate that they be allowed to live? Was it not at your urging that I did not strike them down along with Steffan?

Everything he is saying is true, yet the forbidding chill in his voice, the rigidness of his bearing, makes my own blood run cold. This is a Vlad I have never seen before. The Vlad of old that made his enemies quake with fear.

You do not need me to make this happen, I say. *You have two excellent collaborators inside who await your bidding. You know the plan. The three of you could handle a dozen vampires on your own.*

Vlad crosses the ground between us before I can say another word. *You will not fight for us?*

I was willing to fight for you, I snap back. *You lied to me about your intentions from the start. I am not a part of this battle, Vlad. If I become involved, I become a part of your family. I can't do that. I told you.*

And what of the debt you owe me? Vlad whispers. *I saved Frey for you from Steffan. I brought your niece's friend home. I have let you live as a vampire among us. Do you not owe me something?*

I knew no matter how I answered, it would not satisfy Vlad. I also knew I would have lost Fray had Vlad not saved him from Steffan's attack. That Trish might be home now crying over a lost friend if Vlad had not intervened. That the entire human race might be lost if this plan of Steffan's supporters was not stopped now.

I search his face. *If I do this,* I say at last. *It will be the last thing I can do for you. It will mean the end of our friendship. And it can never be known that I was with you when the six are vanquished. You must promise me.*

For a long moment, I think that Vlad might not have heard me. He is staring off again, his eyes clouded, his lips turned down in a frown. When his face clears, he squares his shoulders and steps back from me.

I accept your terms. Your part will remain a secret between the four of us. I will instruct Amélie and Alexander to never speak of it. I will also instruct them that they are to be at your service if you need anything while you remain in France. They will be protectors of you and your family…

His voice drops and I sense something left unsaid. *You are abdicating to them?*

His eyes lock with mine. *There is no longer any reason I should stay in France. After tonight, I will be gone. You, yourself, said they will make excellent leaders. They have the compassion and human touch that I lack. It makes sense.*

It's almost as if Vlad is talking as much to himself as to me. When he is done, he turns abruptly and goes back into the house. I don't follow him. I have a feeling he is telling Amélie and Alexander the same things he just told me.

When they emerge a few moments later, there is an air of solemnity about the couple that wasn't there before.

They have accepted Vlad's proposal.

He mounts his Ducati and rides away. The three of us go back to the house to await the hour when we will lay in wait for the six who would change the world.

TWELVE

THE NIGHT IS CLOUDLESS AND CRYSTAL CLEAR.
There is no moon to break the darkness that swallows up
the vineyard or to cast even the faintest shadow on the road.
Amélie, Alexander and I are in place on the roof, lying flat,
relying on our senses to alert us to anything approaching.

We have been here an hour. After thirty minutes, others
arrive. They are using the moonless night to shield themselves
among the vines. But we know they are here. The five who
would plot to kill Vlad. They are not so powerful as Vlad, or
even the three of us, because they have no awareness of our
presence while we know exactly where each is located.

We don't communicate among ourselves, keeping our
thoughts tightly locked away. My blood sings with anticipation. Now that I have committed to the fight, I am ready. It's
been a long time since I tasted the blood of another vampire.
Years. Back to the time when I worked as an enforcer for The
Watchers and one of my duties was to execute rogues.

It was not a duty that I enjoyed, but this, in its way, is no different. Protecting humanity sometimes necessitates drastic action. I am armed tonight as I was then, with only a knife and my blood lust.

The car arrived a few minutes after midnight, a big off-road vehicle that plowed through my dad's vineyards, mowing down rows of old-growth grape vines in its path.

I wondered what my father would think when he saw it. I rage at myself for not thinking it through when I offered the old wine press building as a meeting place. It was remote, true, but the fact that at least two of the vampires would be approaching in a car rather than walking in as the rest of us had done never crossed my mind.

Car doors opened. Vlad got out on the front passenger side. Renaldo, opened the left rear passenger door and stepped out. The driver reversed the car and pulled back the way he had come, incurring even more damage. I gritted my teeth as I watched.

Vlad and Renaldo approached the building. From the roof, I watched with Amélie and Alexander for any sign of movement from the vampires hiding in the vineyard.

There was none.

We listened as the conversation drifted upward to us from the ventilation pipe.

Vlad spoke first. "I am here, Renaldo. As you requested. But I must warn you, I can think of nothing you can say that will change my mind about you. Or make me accede to your plan."

Renaldo clucked his tongue. "How unfair of you. To dismiss us out of hand. You were once a feared warrior, brutal in the defense of those under your command. But now, when you command the most fearsome creatures to walk the earth, you are content to let us dwell in the shadows. To live as scavengers when we should all be living as kings."

"And how long would those kingdoms last? Once you subjugated mortals, what would come next? Vampires are a lazy lot, content to take mortal pleasures. Those pleasures would die away with the humans."

"You do not think we could become a race of innovators on our own? Why do you think so little of us? Steffan did not."

"Steffan was an ego-maniac. Once you did his bidding, he would get rid of you, one by one, until his was the only 'kingdom' left standing. The world would become a bleak place. One I would not care to inhabit."

There was a pause. We could hear Renaldo pacing the room. "Then," he said at last, "It's a good thing you will not be around to suffer it."

He signaled telepathically to the vampires hidden among the vines. Unfortunately for him, we hear his signal, too. The three of us jump soundlessly from our hiding place and go to meet the vampires rising from the vineyards. They are not expecting to see anyone, especially three powerful vampires appearing before them like specters. Amélie and Alexander take the three to our right. I take the two to our left.

Renaldo's vampires were all relatively new and while they expected to be able to take one vampire, even an old, powerful one like Vlad, they were caught completely off guard by us. I grab the first vampire's head and twist until I hear vertebrae pop. He drops. I will finish this one off after I take care of the second.

He is older and squares off against me with a snarl. We circle each other until I grow tired of the game and lunge. I catch him with a hand against the back of his neck. He fumbles for a knife in his belt. I get it first and slash at his throat. The first spilled blood unleashes the beast. I grip his head and pull his neck toward me, latching onto to the wound with my mouth. He struggles but only for a short time. As his blood becomes mine, his life flashes in my head. It was a life of brutality, beyond redemption. I feel no remorse when blood turns to salty, bitter water. He is gone. I let his body fall to the ground.

The second vampire is struggling to his feet, his head in his hands as he tried to straighten his neck. A piece of vine lay at my feet. I pick it up and plunge it into his chest. He collapses in on himself, his head still at that odd angle, but now, his hands scrabble for the stake in his heart. I hear the beating stop and his blood cease to flow. I think of drinking from him, too, but the first kill gave me enough to sustain nightmares for a month. I do not want to take on this one's transgressions, too.

I turn to Amélie and Alexander. Two vampires lay dead at their feet and they are drinking from the third. I watch until they are finished, their eyes glowing yellow at me when they stand.

Everything happened silently and was over in minutes. We move as one toward the building. When we sweep the curtain inside, it's to greet a startled Reynaldo, who was expecting a sight far different than that of three blood stained, snarling vampires smelling of his vanquished friends.

THIRTEEN

REYNALDO GASPS AND WHIRLS TO FACE VLAD, his face gone white, his hands shaking. His thoughts project to all of us, first feigning shock that Vlad would have broken his trust by bringing friends. When he reads from our own thoughts and sees what had happened, he protests innocence, saying the others acted alone and not at his bidding.

Vlad says nothing for a long while, letting Reynaldo squirm as his own thoughts are completely sealed off. Finally, he reaches out to me alone.

What is your counsel this time?

I am caught off guard by Vlad's question. I know what I should say, mercy, set a good example, etc. etc. But it's what I said the first time, and that led us here. *You have no choice,* I say sadly. *Do what you must.*

He turns then to Alexander. *As new leader, do you concur we should pronounce the second death on this vampire?*

Alexander steps forward and draws a sword from the folds of his coat. He starts to hand it to Vlad, but Vlad steps back and away.

Reynaldo drops to his knees. *As new sovereign, Alexander, I pledge loyalty to you. Please—*

The sword slices through the air. Reynaldo's head parts from his body, his blood turning to red ash as it hits the air. In a moment, his body bursts into flame.

Then there's nothing left but dust.

Vlad pulls a cell phone from his pocket and sends a message to his driver to come back. I stop him.

"Tell him we will meet him at the road. There has been enough damage done to my father's fields."

"This means—"

I sigh. "I know. This means we will have to carry the bodies out. But I'm not sure how I'm going to explain rows of old-growth vines being destroyed. I can't risk anymore."

He passes the message on to his driver. Then, "I suppose we might as well get it over with," he sighs.

I can only imagine the picture we make, the four of us carrying the dead bodies of five vampires out of the fields. Amélie, Alexander and I each carry one. Vlad has two, one slung over each shoulder. We pile them into the back of the SUV and climb in ourselves. The car reeks of old blood and bile.

Vlad instructs the driver to let me off at my driveway, where I'd left my car, then to take Amélie and Alexander home. When I get out, so does Vlad. He sends the driver away.

I look at him with upturned eyebrows.

He laughs. "Don't worry. I'm not going to ask you to let me spend the night. I just wanted to be alone with you one last time."

It's my turn to chuckle. "I think you once told me that to a vampire, there is no one last time. We have forever, remember?"

"So I did." His expression sobers. "I meant what I said to you, Anna. You are the first woman since my beloved Jusztina—"

"No, Vlad," I say, stopping him. "There is no future for us."

"Not now, maybe." Vlad lets a smile play at the corner of his lips. "But…"

He takes me in his arms before I can resist, and his lips are on mine. His strength is formidable, he's in my head, promising pleasure beyond description. He lets me taste it, feel it in every part of my body before breaking away to leave me wilted and breathless.

"That's not fair," I whisper.

"It wasn't meant to be." He releases me and steps back. "Good-by for now, Anna Strong," he says.

Before I can reply, he's gone.

It takes me awhile to relax enough to fall asleep after Vlad's departure. When I finally do, it's to dream about him and I awake feeling guilty. I realize I've been away from Frey too long. As soon as Trish's play is over, I'll call for my jet to pick me up. First stop, will be to see my husband and son.

I go downstairs, knowing Trish will have already left for school and Dad will be in the fields. I doubt he'll discover the ruined vines for awhile. They are pretty remote. When he does, maybe I'll be gone and won't have to come up with a story or even worse, feign innocence. I'm such a bad liar.

I'm not sure how I'm going to occupy my time these next few weeks. Except for vampires, I have only my family here. Maybe I'll join my father in the fields. Hard work and fresh air may take the edge off a body whose sexual appetites were deliberately awakened by a kiss from a vampire prince. I'm not even tempted to track him down. Who I want is Frey.

When the curtain falls on Trish's acting debut, our house is turned into party central. Dad spares no expense, catered food, a band, open bar. The yard is festooned with lights, excited young actors fill the house with laughter. I watch from the stairway as they come and go, reveling in the knowledge that I played a part in making this happen. A large bouquet of long-stemmed yellow roses is delivered to Trish with the inscription, "Congratulations on a stunning performance. Your faithful friend, Vlad."

Had he been there? Probably. But he kept his distance.

The doorbell rings again soon after the flowers arrived. Since I'm closest, I open it.

"I can't believe I missed the play," a familiar, wonderful, warm voice greets me. "But the flight got held up in—"

It's as far as Frey gets. I'm in his arms, swallowing up his words in a breathless kiss. I pull him in.

"Where's John-John?"

"He's with his grandparents. He only has two more weeks of school so—"

Once again, that's as far as he gets. No one has seen him yet and I'm not going to let this opportunity pass. I pull him upstairs and into our bedroom, slamming the door shut behind us and jumping into his arms.

Now, the party can begin...

ABOUT THE AUTHOR

JEANNE STEIN IS THE AWARD WINNING, national bestselling author of the Urban Fantasy series, *The Anna Strong Vampire Chronicles* and the *Fallen Siren* Series written as S. J. Harper. She has thirteen full length books to her credit, several novellas, and numerous short stories, including "The Wolf's Paw", reprinted in Hex Publishers' 2015 anthology, *Nightmares Unhinged*.

OTHER TITLES IN THE
ANNA STRONG, VAMPIRE SERIES

NOVELS:

The Becoming
Blood Drive
The Watcher
Legacy
Retribution
Chosen
Crossroads
Haunted
Blood Bond

NOVELLAS:

Cloud City

Bruce County Public Library
1243 MacKenzie Rd.
Port Elgin, Ontario N0H 2C6

CPSIA information can be obtained
at www.ICGtesting.com
Printed in the USA
LVOW11s2158110517
534222LV00001B/26/P